Daughter's Day B·L·U·E·S

by Laura Pegram

pictures by Cornelius Van Wright and Ying-Hwa Hu

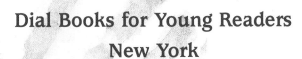

Dial Books for Young Readers
New York

Published by Dial Books for Young Readers
A division of Penguin Putnam Inc.
345 Hudson Street
New York, New York 10014

Designed by Julie Rauer
Printed in Hong Kong on acid-free paper
First Edition
1 3 5 7 9 10 8 6 4 2

Library of Congress Cataloging in Publication Data
Pegram, Laura.
Daughter's Day blues/by Laura Pegram;
pictures by Cornelius Van Wright and Ying-Hwa Hu.—1st ed.
p. cm.
Summary: Phyllis Mae thinks that her little brother gets too much attention,
so her Nana and Momma decide to have a special Daughter's Day celebration.
ISBN 0-8037-1557-9
[1. Brothers and sisters—Fiction. 2. Grandmothers—Fiction.
3. Afro-Americans—Fiction.] I. Van Wright, Cornelius, ill. II. Hu, Ying-Hwa, ill. III. Title.
PZ7.P3582Dau 2000 [E]—DC20 94-41555 CIP AC

The art was prepared using watercolors and pencils on illustration board.

For my nieces, Monique and Imani,
as I celebrate them,
and for my mother, Phyllis Mae

L.P.

To Jon and Rita

C.V.W. and Y.H.H.

J.T. was sticking the candles into the chocolate when he slipped off the chair. He wasn't hurt, but the Mother's Day cake was smashed. "Nana told you to stop," I said, "but you have such a hard head. Now look at the cake!" J.T. started bawling and Nana rushed to pick him up. My little brother J.T., well, he's just plain spoiled.

I picked up my puppet, Little Sis, and left Nana and J.T. in the kitchen. Then I leaned against Momma's favorite chair. I wished she were still here. Momma and Nana had opened their gifts quickly because Momma had to be at work by three. Now ribbons and bows were all around the floor. When I saw the pretty purple one, I stuck it on my knee. Then I helped Little Sis into a split.

J.T. had settled down, so Nana began to pick up the party paper. When I asked if she could do a split just like Little Sis, Nana shook her head and laughed. She kneeled, and pointed at the bow on my knee.

"Phyl," she said, "did you know that your knee is the very best place for a bow to be?"

"Why, Nana?" I giggled.

"Because you're a gift to me—you and J.T."

"Was I wrapped up all in ribbons when I was born?" I asked.

"No, but you had a headful of hair and you fit right into the crook of my arm. J.T. too. Now look at you," she said with a smile.

Nana was about to put a ribbon in my hair when J.T. ran over holding his pants and doing his little dance. Nana took him to the bathroom.

"Nana," I said when she came back, "is there a day for daughters like the one for mothers?"

Nana smiled. Then she picked up the calendar that we had made together. "Here we go, Phyl," she said. "Daughter's Day is just around the corner, seven days from today."

"Can we make a cake like today, only put it out of J.T.'s way?"

"Yes, baby," she said. "And how about some banana pancakes for breakfast?"

"Yeah! And after, can you show me how to whistle? My friend Nikki knows how."

"Phyllis Mae, it'll be your day." Nana laughed and gave me a long squeeze. "Why don't we make your puppet some company too?"

I scooped up Little Sis. "With curly purple hair just like hers. Oh, Nana, I can't wait!"

The next day in the park I was on the jungle gym with Nikki. "Guess what?" I said. "Nana, Momma, and I are going to celebrate Daughter's Day."

"There's no such thing," Nikki said.

"There is so," I said. "We're having a party with cake and everything. Nana said you can come."

"Well, Daughter's Day is silly, but you know I like cake," Nikki said as she jumped off the bars. "And cookies, and cream," she shouted at me as she ran toward the tire swing. "Even if it is a make-believe day."

"It's not a make-believe day," I said to myself.

Nikki joined two sisters on the swing and then whistled for me. "Come on, Phylly—we can both fit," she cried. But just then I didn't feel like fitting in.

Each day after that, Nana, J.T., and I did something for the party. And each day J.T. got into some kind of trouble. On Tuesday we bought party supplies. J.T. toppled a tower of party hats. On Wednesday we bought things for the cake. J.T. dropped the eggs on the sidewalk. On Saturday we bought balloons from the lady in the park. J.T. promised to hold on tight, but . . . I wondered what would happen next.

On Daughter's Day morning I woke up early. It was raining outside, but I didn't care. Nothing would spoil this day. I left my brother in bed with the covers over his head. But the minute I got into the bathroom, there he was knocking at the door. When I opened it, J.T. was doing his potty dance barefoot in front of me.

"Today is Daughter's Day," I said.

"Gotta go," he said, pushing past me. I went to my room and put on the party dress Momma had laid out for me. Momma had gone to work early so she'd be home for the party.

When I went into the kitchen, J.T. was running out. The floor felt sticky under my feet and Nana was standing by the stove spooning out oatmeal.

"What about my pancakes?" I said.

Nana turned to me and said, "I'm sorry, baby, but J.T. knocked over the maple syrup. We'll have pancakes tomorrow."

I sat down hard in the chair and moved my spoon around slowly in the thick cereal.

I was pouting and playing with Little Sis when Nana started mixing butter and sugar in a big bowl. Nana said nothing, but I knew what she was doing. She was fixing to make my Daughter's Day cake.

"Can I do one?" I asked when she began adding the eggs. "I'll be a good egger."

Nana smiled and tied her apron around me. "Tap it gently, Phyl," she said.

I tapped it twice. The egg plopped into the bowl and the sun spilled open.

"That's my girl," Nana said, picking the shells from the bowl with her fingers and handing me the fork.

Everything was going fine until J.T. came in. Nana let him butter the pan. J.T. greased the cake pan one minute, his hair the next. Then he ate the butter. "Oh, no!" I said.

"J.T.!" Nana said, shaking her head. "Now I've got to clean you up."

I could hear J.T. splashing in the tub. "Little Sis," I said, "he'll *never* get out of the water."

Nana was drying J.T. off when the phone rang. I ran to get it and he was right behind me.

"Momma called to talk to me," I said.

J.T. started crying and coughing and running his nose. I gave him the phone and all he talked about was eating butter and diving in the tub. By the time he finished, the telephone cord was wrapped around both of us and Momma had to get back to work.

"J.T.," I yelled, "this is Daughter's Day! Not a day for sons!" I ran down the hall into my bedroom and slammed the door. J.T. was spoiling my day. He always gets his way. I hugged my puppet and put my head deep into my pillow and cried myself to sleep.

The rain on the window woke me up. It was lightning too. I rubbed my eyes hard because I thought I was dreaming. There on the radiator was a cake and a card. On the front of the card was a little girl with a purple bow on her knee and a puppet in her hand.

I was staring so hard, I didn't even hear Momma's footsteps when she came in. "Happy Daughter's Day," she said, giving me a big hug and a kiss. "Ready to make puppets?"

Nikki, Nana, and J.T. were waiting for me in the front room.

"Looks like Little Sis could use a friend or two," said Nana as she picked sewing strings out of her basket. Nikki started whistling and cutting. I tried to whistle too. Only wind came out at first. Then a sound. A soft breezy sound. At first I thought it was the storm outside, but Nana said it was me.

I ran to the mirror to see if I could make another whistle. Momma lit the cake and everyone gathered around. Nana said that if I had any air left, I could blow out the candles.

"Daughter's Day *is* a great idea," said Nikki. "Now make a wish so we can cut the cake!"

I took a deep breath and made my lips into a kiss. I blew out all of the candles but one. J.T. and Nikki leaned over to help me blow out that last one and then came the sound again. J.T. clapped and Nana winked at me. This time it was clear even to me that the whistle—and the day—was all mine.

E   Pegram, Laura.
Pegram
            Daughter's Day
            blues.

Black Experience

DATE			

#15.99

E   Pegram, Laura.
Pegram
            Daughter's Day
            blues.

BAKER & TAYLOR